TIME SLIP

BESTSELLING AUTHOR OF STONE AGE
M.L. BANNER

TIME
SLIP

M.L. BANNER

ASIN: B00TF0J3I6 (eBook)
ISBN: 0-9908741-6-8 (Paperback)
First Edition: 03/2015
Second Edition: 02/2017

Time Slip is an original work of fiction.
The characters, events, and dialog are the products of this author's
vivid imagination. Any similarity to real persons, living, dead, or
undead, is purely coincidental and not intended by the author.
Most of the science and historical incidents described in this novel
are based on reality; the rest is fictional.

Cover Art: Demonza
Editors: Karen Conlin & Vonda at First Editing

Published by

Toes in the Water Publishing, LLC
www.toesinthewaterpublishing.com

The Stone Age World
An apocalyptic solar storm takes the world into a new Stone Age
"A great apocalyptic story!"

Stone Age (Volume #1) – The Event caught all but a few by surprise

DESOLATION (Volume #2) – Survival is the only option during the new Stone Age

CICADA (Volume #3) – No safety in a post-apocalyptic world

REMNANTS (Volume #4) – Coming Soon

Stone Age Shorts
Short novels set in the Stone Age World

Max's Epoch –Find out what happens to Stone Age's favorite Character, Max Thompson
(Exclusively available @ www.mlbanner.com/free)

Time Slip – A scientist attempts to use a slip in time to save his wife, but ends up in a new Stone Age

Songs of a Dead Country – A survivalist fights to live and find his way in a new Stone Age

Want more about the Stone Age World?
www.StoneAgeSeries.com
Stone Age World facts vs. fiction; what's next; extra material not in the books; more.

Thanks and Acknowledgments

To my friend Jeffry: I will miss our time together every Wednesday discussing life, your music, and my stories. Until we see each other again in our heavenly home.

To my wife Lisa: thank you for enduring the endless days that I spend in other worlds, away from you, and for always being willing to read and review my work so enthusiastically.

A special note to David, one of my readers, who lost his wife Amy to a horrible illness: I know you would do anything to get her back. You're in my prayers.

Finally, thanks to all my readers. I hope you enjoyed this one.

"I'll give you all I got to give if you say you'll love me too.
I may not have a lot to give but what I got I'll give to you.
I don't care too much for money, money can't buy me love."
~ *Can't Buy Me Love*, Lennon – McCartney

Chapter 1
Aug 7 (01:15)

A simple pop, barely audible above the machine's clamorous roar, unceremoniously confirmed for the third time man's greatest scientific achievement: the creation of a doorway to another time. There was no celebratory pomp, no parade of reporters, not even a throng of scientists to witness this feat. There was only Dr. Ron, its creator, watching with the same detached wonderment he'd experienced the first two times.

Just forty hours earlier, he had accidentally created a time slip. It was supposed to have been a simple day of testing, a day that began without his wife/assistant, who was home resting from a cold that wouldn't go away. But he hadn't been about to let this opportunity pass, after the mountains of red tape necessary to get the imprimatur from ERCOT and the university. With the dated waiver in hand to pull an abnormal amount of power from the grid on that day, and the next scheduled waiver over a month away, he had gone ahead and run the first test himself. The five-minute warm-up routine

ran as expected. What was completely unexpected was the vortex
generated by the machine. At first, he was mesmerized by this
spinning ethereal form, concentric circles of bluish light, like some
round, mystic throw rug suspended above and perpendicular to the
floor. In the center of this was a muddy image of another laboratory,
not too dissimilar from his; seeing it was like looking through a dirty
window. Then it had occurred to him that this might not be just a
window for viewing some other place; it could be a doorway. Then it
had closed.

He remembered his excitement as he had run to his side
office and grabbed a prized Christmas gift from his grandnephew: a
remote-controlled drone and its controller. The drone had a
camera—maybe it would feed images remotely to his computer. He
had added the electronic thermometer sensor from outside the lab
window, and about twenty minutes and a few test flights later, he was
adept enough to try sending it through, if that proved possible.

The second time he had fired up the machine, the drone had
already been airborne—like now. That time he had been nervous,
unsure the anomaly could be re-created. Yet the window had popped
open and he had flown the drone into it. The drone almost
immediately lurched up, as if it hit a headwind, and then crashed. He
had eyed the remote and wondered, *Did I do that?* Ten seconds after
opening, the doorway had closed on the dead drone and the other
world it now occupied—but not before transmitting some data.

Then yesterday, his data had led him to believe it was a
doorway to another time. So he had planned this next test, anxious
not only because this could confirm his theory, but also because this
time he would be knowingly breaking the law for only the second
time in his life (the first had been a parking violation at the U): a civil

statute governing the use of power. He figured though the risk was worth the reward: if he could prove this really was a way to create a controlled time slip, he would change the world.

Now, with the doorway open and the ten-second clock started, he didn't hesitate steering the drone toward the opening. This time it was no Radio Shack toy: based on a military design now available for commercial and research operations, this drone was fitted with multiple sensors, cameras, and top of the line electronics—hardened against electromagnetic pulses and equipped with miniaturized radio equipment and so much more than he probably needed, which explained the ridiculously high price tag. Thankfully, he had almost limitless funds. Besides, what was a few dollars when you were changing the world?

He glanced at the computer from his periphery to confirm that all the sensors were transmitting data. Everything was a go. He looked back up and his heart stopped.

It was him. He was looking at himself on the other side of the doorway. His other self had just pulled a slat from a boarded-up window. He watched himself look outside. Then his other self spun around and stared directly at him, seemingly just as startled as he was. There was no doubt he was looking at his own image. He practically leapt, startled, certainly from the spine-tingling paradox but also from the realization that he hadn't been paying attention to the drone. Then the window closed, and he was staring at the area where the doorway had been—and a beat-up hundred-thousand-dollar drone.

He was now certain of two facts, and he didn't need the drone to confirm them: the window he created was definitely a time slip to an undetermined future, and he was going to travel through it.

What he didn't know was why.

Chapter 2
Aug 7 (09:10)

"I'm afraid it's inoperable glioblastoma multiforme, a nasty form of brain cancer," Dr. Peter Valdez said over his spectacles. His cheeks were rosy, his eyes puffy and bloodshot. He pressed his palms together under his desk and wished he were anywhere but here.

"Is there nothing we can do?" Dr. Ron pleaded; his eyes were dams about to burst.

Valdez hesitated. "Chemo is an option, but that would only delay the inevitable, and she'd be sick from the chemo." He paused before continuing, choking back his emotions. "I'm sorry, but the only potential treatment for this type of cancer is five to ten years away, and Betsy has only a few months."

"Few months?" he whispered, barely above his breath. The weight of this statement was unthinkable, unbearable. Ron couldn't fathom a life without her.

"What happens in five to ten years?" Ron asked, detached, only half listening now. His shoulders slumped, body slouched in his chair.

Valdez thought about what he wanted to say, making sure he said it correctly the first time. "There is a company called Cancer Bio-Systems that has come up with a miraculous drug combination that could cure your wife's form of cancer. However, it is at least a year or two from human trials and then another three to five years before the FDA could possibly approve it for general release to the public. This is the only treatment with any potential on the horizon. The damnable thing is they may have this thing licked, based on what I hear from a friend who is on their research team. Only Betsy doesn't have that long." Now he was angry. "Dammit, Ron, if there was any way I could think of to beg, borrow, or steal this drug for Betsy or keep her alive long enough till we knew, I would. But I've thought this through every which way till Sunday, and I just don't have an alternative."

Ron knew this was Pete's plain way of telling him the way it was. It wasn't because they were related—he was just as direct with all of his patients. Every word that came out of his mouth was meant exactly as it was said, but with a Texas regionalism thrown in for color. At this time though, he wasn't sure if he longed for a physician who beat around the bush, afraid to spell out what everyone knew. No, Pete was exactly what they needed.

Then Ron sat straight up as if he had received a jolt of electricity. Now alert, he asked very slowly, "Are you sure about this company, that is, as sure as you can be?"

"I would stake my reputation on it."

"You were a research scientist for years before you turned to private practice, right?"

"You know this to be true." Pete's brows furrowed, his eyes

curiously examining his friend of thirty-three years.

"Think about this before you answer, because I am deadly serious when I ask it..."

"I'm listening." He stared at Ron sternly.

"If you knew what this company was using, and if I gave you the okay to move forward with administering the formula even though it would be against the law because it was not fully tested, would you administer this to my wife?"

"Since you know the answer to this most obvious question as well, I'm wondering why you are even asking."

"I'm asking, because I want to be sure of your answer."

Pete considered. "Since you are asking me and you know my answer, I can only assume that you are planning something irrational and risky," he said, thinking his brother-in-law might try to steal the formula.

It was Ron's turn to scowl now. "Since when have I done anything that anyone would qualify as irrational?"

"That's what scares the hell out of me."

"So answer the question."

"Okay, fine. You know I woul--will do whatever it takes to save your wife, my sister, from the ravages of this disease."

"Great, so do what you can to keep her alive and strong enough for the next twelve months or so. And give me all the details of this company."

~~~

About ten minutes later, Betsy stepped through the door of Dr. Valdez's reception area. Ron looked up from his palms and welcomed her with a smile. He acted as if he just arrived, too, as if Pete and he hadn't already worked out all the details of the consultation that was about to follow.

"The doctor will see you now," said the receptionist.

Betsy squeezed his hand hard, and he squeezed back. "It will be all right, Bets, I promise."

Chapter 3
Aug 9 (07:55)

Dr. Montgomery "Monty" Merriweather walked in through the solid and very plain public entrance door. The reception room was equally utilitarian, with a single desk void of any work and one secretarial chair behind it, a warehouse tag hung from its side announcing its lack of use or its recent purchase. Dr. Ron's reputation for utility over form was legendary in the University circles. Unlike most male professors, he would never have had a pretty female student assisting him, unless she happened to also be the smartest in her class. So Monty expected to be processed by someone resembling an elderly librarian in a lab coat, gray hair in a bun, angry eyes glaring through wire-rimmed glasses perched on a crooked nose. He smiled at the thought. There was no one here. No one at all.

He had never been *here* before, which seemed ironic because he had contributed to the collider's design—a pretty central piece, in fact. Monty wasn't put off by this though, as he knew his friend simply relished the secrecy and promised him a full show of the collider when it was ready. Of course, that had been years ago. Then last night, out of the blue, he got a phone call from his friend, who he hadn't talked to in months, pleading with him to come down to the lab and help him with some tests on the new collider. Luckily the timing was perfect, as Monty's schedule was pretty empty until his next design contract started in a week, followed by one class, MECH3305 – Computer-Aided Engineering Design, which he taught in the fall.

He probably should have been pissed to have been kept in the dark all this time, or should not have said "yes" so quickly to Dr. Ron's pleas, but this was how his friend operated. And to be angry at his behavior would have been just as silly as being angry with the sun for not rising an hour earlier because you wanted it that way.

He heard music in the laboratory.

"So Dr. Stoneridge says it's okay to come in? Wonderful! Thank you!" Monty said effusively to the empty desk and pushed through one of the two doors that led into the lab.

Paul McCartney belted out *Can't Buy Me Love* but the reverb seemed exaggerated, most likely because of the room's enormous size. He stepped onto a metal grate walkway and gawked at the giant space. He was standing on a ten-foot-wide mezzanine surrounding a cavernous sunken laboratory, close to a football field in length. He continued to the railing, noting his position was near what he'd call the fifty-yard line, and looked down.

"Wow!" There it was: Dr. Ron's collider. It was a thing of beauty. A giant metal tube ran the length of the entire building, with an opening near the center, like some high-tech drain pipe that had been separated in the middle. Monty noticed its curvature as the tube vanished through the walls at each end. Even though the circumference was smaller than that of most non-linear particle colliders, it was still impressive when one stood over it.

He noticed that Dr. Ron was sitting at a computer workstation directly in front of the cut-out, looking up at him. "Monty," he hollered after the song concluded, "are you going to just stand there, or are you coming down to help me?"

"Be right down," Monty yelled back and trotted down the stairs as John and Paul sang *Any Time At All* at the tops of their lungs.

~~~

"You're kidding... Right?" Monty looked at his friend with a smile, sure he was the recipient of some elaborate practical joke. Dr. Ron described what had transpired since they last saw each other, not leaving much out. Then, on the third aromatic cup of coffee from the Keurig, he got around to explaining the results of his first test, omitting his suppositions and assumptions, and launched right into the results of the second test. He never told Monty about the third time he opened the doorway and saw himself.

Monty's demeanor never changed through the entire story, as if he were waiting for the punchline of a long joke, until he looked at the data--and then he saw the facts.

"You actually created a stable vortex?"

"I didn't say that. It lasts for only"—he pointed to a notation on one of the loose pages of notes strewn on the work table—"9.99 seconds, repeating."

"So tell me why you're sure this isn't a window to the past?" Monty asked. His mind, like every philosopher or sci-fi theorist, wondered about the possibilities.

"I don't believe it's possible to go to the past. Not only is it not supported by any of our current theories; I believe it's impossible because of the paradoxes we have all posited with backward time travel. Such as, if you went back in time and met yourself, what would happen to the two of you who occupy the same space?"

"Or my favorite," Monty added, "if the future-you killed your father, how could you have been born to do the killing?"

"Exactly!" Dr. Ron held up his index finger. "This is a paradox that cannot be resolved. For all these reasons, I believe you can only travel forward."

"Still, this is amazing. Why haven't I heard about this?" Monty looked around, and then thought of the empty reception area. The words leapt out of his mouth, "You haven't told anyone yet... so why me?"

"Betsy is my usual assistant, but she's at home..." He paused and tightened up, putting on an emotionless mask. "...sick, and I want someone I trust on this who isn't my wife to verify the results before I publish. So, will you help me run the next test?"

"I wouldn't miss it for the world." Monty's gaze followed his friend to the computer station, where without hesitation, he tapped the computer keyboard's Enter key and the machine hummed to life in response.

"That's what I thought," Dr. Ron said with a smile.

"Based on what Einstein postulated this must take a ton of power, far more than just what the accelerator requires." Monty shot a look up to the ceiling's giant power cables. His eyes closed for just a second, enough time to do the mental calculations. "How the hell did you get the okay to pull power from the grid?"

"I didn't."

Chapter 4
Aug 9 (19:23)

Simon Ransacker punched the number on his desk phone, and heard it ringing on the other end. He waited for an answer, impatiently gnawing on his cigar.

The other end picked up, and the recording began playing immediately. "Thank you for calling the laboratory of Stoneridge Research. If you're calling during laboratory hours, we are busy changing the world. Please leave a message—"

He slammed the phone down, severing the connection.

For the fourth time in as many days, the Dallas-Fort Worth grid had almost gone down. The first two times occurred the morning of the 5th, and the third in the wee hours of the 7th, and those had been somewhat of a mystery. Earlier today, his team traced these to the University of Texas and some research being done there. They had received the okay from ERCOT for a one-time draw from the grid, but the other one on the 5th and the one two days later were unsanctioned. Plus, they certainly had underestimated their power usage in their waiver proposal. Then, twelve hours ago, another power drain, worse than the other three, pulled over 50% of the entire grid's power. This time his team had a name to pin on the guilty party: Dr. Ronald Stoneridge. And this time Stoneridge had gone too far. It was one thing to exceed the limit during a research project and extend the research past the end-time specified on the waiver. It was another to blatantly break the law, like that jerk just did. "And on one of the hottest days of the summer… That just chaps my hide." He threw his half-chewed cigar against the wall.

Now that he knew who the culprit was, he wanted to confront him before going to the authorities. He wanted to know what this Dr. Stoneridge was doing with all this power. More important now, he had to stop him from taking any more before the stupid bastard brought the entire Dallas-Fort Worth grid down.

"You are in for a shit-storm now, my friend," Ransacker grinned while banging in the phone number of the person who would bring this shit-storm down on top of Dr. Stoneridge.

"Ransacker? That you?" yelled the voice on the other end.

"Sir, we have a 52% power drain caused by some crazy scientist at UT who doesn't have waivers. Do I have your authority to call the DPD Chief and cut him off before he brings the grid down?"

"Sonofabitch! Are you sure Ransacker?"

"Yes, sir. I'm 100% sure."

"Who is it?"

"A Doctor Ronald Stoneridge from Stoneridge Research."

A long silence was broken by the sound of the phone on the other end being dropped.

"Sir, are you all right?"

"Eh, yah, I'm here. Better give me the details then. I'll make the call. Good work, Ransacker."

"Thank you, sir."

Chapter 5
Aug 9 (21:10)

"Yes." The man who had no name answered his cell and lowered the volume of Mozart's Requiem in D Minor so he could hear better.

"I need you to speed up the job," said a hurried voice filled with nervous energy.

"When?"

"Tonight!"

"My price just doubled, then." The man tossed that out immediately.

The other person hesitated for just a moment. "Money's no object. Just get it done."

"The doctor will be removed tonight, then."

"And the data from his computers?"

"As agreed."

"Fine. Just be sure—"

The man ended the conversation with a click and tossed his phone onto his bedside table.

"Continue, but be quick. I have to work tonight," he told the prostitute, who smiled at him, and then fixed her gaze downward and hurriedly unzipped his pants.

The man responded with an extra measure of pressure on the remote's volume up button. The sonorous voices of the choir filled every space of his hotel room. They reached climax with their "Amen", just before he did.

Chapter 6
Aug 9 (21:20)

"You want to do what?" Monty bellowed almost hysterically. Dr. Ron and he had just completed their analysis of the drone's data. It operated perfectly and sent back almost a terabyte of data. After seeing the portal in person and reviewing the data, it seemed conclusive enough: they really could generate a time portal, or what Dr. Ron referred to as a time slip to the future. That's when Dr. Ron told Monty his immediate plans to go forward in time to save his Betsy.

"We're going to send me forward in time by five years. Then you're going to send another drone forward in approximately three months, and maybe one more—assuming you have time—another three months after that. With a little luck, one of those two times, I will find a way to get you the information Betsy's physician will need."

"You mean a cure for her cancer?"

"Yes."

"Aside from the obvious moral problems with what you are asking me to do, how do you expect to come back?" As soon as Monty asked this, he realized the answer: his friend wasn't coming back.

"You know this is a one-way trip since we established that you can only move forward in time."

"So, all of this about needing someone to provide testimony before you publish your paper is crap, isn't it? You just need me to be your messenger boy, to communicate with your brother-in-law for you."

"You know it's more than that." Ron's voice rose as desperation set in; without Monty's help, the plan wouldn't work. "Yes, this is the real reason I asked you to join me in these experiments. I not only needed someone I could trust, I needed someone to send in the probes, and..."

"...deal with the consequences, like the police, who you said would probably be coming soon to shut this down?"

"Monty, I am really sorry to throw this on you, but I have no other choice. And if I have to--"

"Dammit Ron, don't even say it or you're going to piss me off more than I already am. I know you know me well enough. So regardless of what I say, you're going to jump through, knowing that I'll be forced to help you or your jump will be for nothing and I will be in some way responsible for your wife's death."

The two men sat in silence, looking at the work table, covered with printouts and their pages of notes.

"So how do you know this will work?"

Dr. Ron considered divulging the images he had seen of himself earlier, images he had removed from the data he had shown

Monty, but decided against it. Monty was already on board. They needed to take the next step.

"Because it has to," he finally answered.

Chapter 7
Aug 9 (23:05)

Dr. Ron pressed "Enter" and the machine came to life for a fifth time, humming through a precise warmup cycle, surging from a thump-thump-thump beat into a mighty rumble. It sounded to him like some massive primeval lion whose morning yawn gradually increased in cadence until it became a thunderous roar. His own heartbeat followed in sync to the rhythm of the collider, waiting for the machine to reach its apex. When his heart was practically leaping out of his chest, the doorway into another time opened, and without hesitation, he stepped into it.

"Amazing" fell from his lips, an unheard whisper not because of loud noises but a complete absence of sound immediately upon entering the slip. Little pins of brightness surrounded and accelerated toward him, slowly at first and then speeding up. After a few moments, thousands of pins were rushing at him from all directions. Then his world was awash in millions of white laser beams—pins of light with long tails, a glittering spectral blast of luminescence. It reminded him of the sparkling diamond-like glitter of a seascape at sunset, but a thousand times that and all at once. There was so much brightness he had to shield his eyes. *Should have worn sunglasses*, he thought. It wasn't like he could use this information again: it was a one-way trip into the future.

An enormous flash erupted everywhere at once: a brightness that would have put a lightning strike to shame. Then, for just a moment, it was completely black, an absolute absence of light. If it were possible, it was as if every atom of light was being sucked out of the world around him. *Am I actually witnessing the infamous dark matter?* His thoughts carried no further before his stomach turned and ended up in his throat as weightlessness consumed him, like on the Racer, a roller coaster at Kings Island from his childhood memories. Even though he had almost puked each time, he loved it so much that he had ridden the damn thing twenty-seven times.

Then the feeling was gone, instantly replaced with a wave of emotions. It was the strangest of feelings; he was experiencing the emotions of a thousand different events at once. Each emotion was attached to an image or group of images --seemingly disjointed memories from another person's life, or were they his? It was a life's worth of movies in an instant. His brain ached and exhaustion consumed him; it was far worse than any multi-nighter research binge.

Then the weightlessness and flood of information abruptly stopped and everything around him was still and black.

As if he were in a dining room in which the dimmer switch was being turned up slowly to reveal the main course, he could start to see. *Perhaps my personal space and time are catching up with this future space and time?* Within a span of a few seconds his surroundings looked...

normal.

He had a suspicion and turned around to confirm it. His assistant, Monty, was nowhere to be seen. There was no doorway to that place in time he had just come from--just a muddy blur where he stepped through, a distortion, but nothing more. Suspecting that Monty could see him through this one-way window in time, Dr. Ron gave him the thumbs-up. Then, as if on command, the blur disappeared. Ten seconds! Yet for him, at least two minutes had passed. His head hurt more as he considered this. He had work to do.

The space around him looked familiar, yet very different.

They had reasoned that he would end up five to ten years into the future, but at some unknown location; it could be down the street or in Poland, for all he knew. They could only assume he was years into the future—that was his hope anyway. Their data had confirmed three assumptions: this was some sort of laboratory similar to his own; it was ruined, damaged by some event they couldn't possibly foresee—they just didn't have the time to run more tests; and they knew that radiation increased the farther forward in the future they went. This final point they assumed had to do with the timing of their time slips, suspecting that they were looking at some point on the calendar farther along in the summer—albeit years ahead, when solar radiation levels would be greater.

The nausea finally passed, so he decided to take his first steps in this future world. He immediately had a sense of what the first astronauts must have felt like landing on the moon; it was at once both scary and exhilarating. There was very little light in this space, as there were no overheads and the natural light was mostly blocked by the boards covering the lab's elevated window. He walked directly to it, tripping over debris along the way, intending to rip a board off and allow more light into this space. The debris included both drones he had sent previously, a little banged up, but otherwise untouched.

He yanked with both hands, poking his right hand with one of the hanging nails in the process. *Should have gotten a tetanus booster last time I was in to see Pete.* A creaking bray as the last nail gave up its fight, and the light poured in like a springtime flood. He saw it right away, between the slats, just outside the window: the billboard he had stared at for years, its advertisement changing every few months. Today, or rather the day he left in the past, the advertisement was— or had been?--exactly the same as he saw it now: a topless model, her back to her onlookers, with skin-tight blue jeans temptingly being pulled off by another woman. "But that can't be, unless…" Words leapt out of his mouth as he pivoted in one motion and was hit at once with complete realization.

"It couldn't be," he mumbled out loud, his mouth agape.

This was his laboratory.

Chapter 8
Aug 9 (23:10)

Monty watched Dr. Ron step into the time window, but it was far more surreal than him merely stepping through a window frame: he watched him step into a reality TV program, but through the television. Monty observed his friend look around first before Ron turned and gave him the thumbs up. Then the window disappeared, the machine abruptly stopped, and all the lab's lights went out. Only the computer's drive and the UPS's warning beeps sounded, loud in the silence. Monty's shadow was cast on the floor by the lab's only light, coming from the computer monitor screens. At that moment, the only other sound was a slight ticking from the collider's heated metal surfaces being cooled by liquid nitrogen.

The momentary quiet was shattered by a loud thumping on the outside door. Then he noticed the strobing blue and red lights flashing through the single chin-high basement window facing the highway outside. He *knew* what was coming next.

"This is the Dallas Police Department. Open up. You have

ten seconds or we will break down this door." The voice and banging were somewhat muffled by the door's thickness. This lit a fire under Monty, who blasted out of his seat, grabbed the portable hard drive out of the computer, and pushed on a flat wall panel on the side of the laboratory beneath the stairwell. It gave way and he stepped through the opening into Dr. Ron's hidden office, where they had been earlier. He pushed back against the bookcase, concealing the doorway, and it returned to its place, clicking satisfactorily. At the same time he heard, more faintly, "This is your last chance …"

The room was pitch black, but it didn't take long for him to grope around for the exit and open it, the smell of grass and the hum of crickets immediately filling his senses. Monty ascended a flight of concrete steps with caution, looking around to make sure the police weren't here. The field was dark as well, but he had a loose familiarity with it from their breaks of "fresh air" earlier today. Already his eyes were adjusting, and he could make out the shape of the ellipse and the electrified fence in the distance, where his safest escape route lay. He turned his head back to confirm that the overhead spots were out, and therefore the power, and jogged straight back, over the hump of the ellipse—the only part of the particle accelerator visible to the world--and over the electric security fence. He was thankful it was off and he had parked his car off the road, away from the laboratory and the police.

Chapter 9
Aug 9 (23:50)

The rented Escalade was parked on the side of a frontage road beside a billboard telling highway motorists to buy some brand of blue jeans painted onto some mostly naked model. The vehicle was like some elegant but powerful black animal that had been stalking its prey, the Stoneridge Research Laboratory, and got bored waiting. So it rested, ready to spring when it was time. Its form was barely visible under the dusky light cast from the city's reflections and the evening stars. This entire surrounding area was experiencing a blackout.

The man watched from behind the slick vehicle's dark eyelids; a small flash of light from his lighter was the only indication the Caddy was occupied. Unconcerned about being seen, the man took a deep puff, lowering the side window slightly to let out his exhales. He peered at the scene in front of him, an experienced hunter waiting patiently for his moment to pounce.

The police were looking for the same man he was. Best to let them do his job for him and not get in their way. Sometimes, the police presence forced a target to move. In these cases, watching and waiting always worked best. He took another long drag from his Dunhill, eyes unblinking.

A smoldering anger bubbled up inside him. His handlers hadn't told him police were involved, and he doubted it was a coincidence. It certainly was not a complication he had accounted for when quoting his fee. The simplicity of the job was heavily weighted by his target: a pudgy scientist who did little else aside from testing his research at his lab or spending time at home with his wife, and on a rare occasion teaching a class at the university. He knew his target well, having successfully completed another job for the same handler over a decade ago, involving simply the theft of some "trade secrets about gamma radiation." Now he was back and his target was older and pudgier but better funded this time. This bred complications, but none he hadn't accounted for: increased security and questions about the target's benefactors and their own motives. For all he knew, his own handlers paid for the doctor's research and they wanted a return on their money now; perhaps it was the competition. It really didn't matter who was funding him or what the research was about. He just hated the police being involved.

More arrived, rolling past him with their sirens silent, telling him what he suspected; his target was not here. He could always return if he had to, when there were only one or two officers, to find the data his handler wanted. He would go to the target's home next. Most likely the researcher was on the run and would quickly gather a few things to hide out somewhere. He had to move before he lost his target's scent.

The man took a final drag and flicked his cigarette onto the road as he slowly turned the black predator around, lights still out, and stalked off in the other direction.

Chapter 10
In The Future

What had happened to his lab in just a few short years since he left? Fear started to take hold… Maybe it was much later in the future than they had calculated.

Dr. Ron's mind searched for an answer as he stared at the ruins of what was his laboratory. Time travel was far from an exact science. They had only been guessing that by pushing an increasing amount of power to the collider, the fields would reach light speed quicker, thereby generating a doorway leading farther into the future.

He was now terrified that he had arrived so far into the future that he would have no chance of finding Dr. Mendelson, much less the cure for his wife's cancer. As crazy as his plan must have seemed, failure had never been a consideration. He had just assumed that he would make this work. Now doubt and a nagging fear crept through his veins… and there was something else: the world was silent.

He instinctively reached for his hearing aids, assuming he had turned them off during the machine's noisy routine and forgot to turn them back on. He reached behind his curly hair to the one in his right ear—the one he could better hear from---and switched the on/off back and forth, then did the same with the volume. *Nothing.* He pulled it out and was rewarded with the subdued ambient noises surrounding him: the slight breeze squeezing through the single window slat; the echo of a cricket off in the dark recesses of his lab; a piece of debris sliding farther off a pile he had disturbed a moment ago. His hearing aids must be dead.

He pulled out the other to receive a little more sound, although he hadn't heard much of anything out of that ear since a lab accident took about 70% of his total hearing over a decade before he went though the time slip. Both looked fine but obviously something was wrong. Perhaps more important was his right hand, which he had already forgotten and now was pulsing out a nice flow of blood. Slipping the aids into his pocket, he squeezed his fingers against his damaged palm and held his hand above his head, like one of his students asking to be called on in class.

Time to get down to business, he thought, willing his fear away and focusing on getting to Dr. Mendelson's lab. Dr. Ron touched his inside back pocket and confirmed the presence of the paper containing Dr. Gregory Mendelson's information. He stepped gingerly over and around the debris, navigating his way to his side office door to get the keys to the facility's truck and drive to Mendelson's laboratory. His gaze swept around his own lab to find a clue as to what may have happened.

The two ends of the accelerating tubes looked completely intact. But the area beyond this appeared to have been damaged by an explosion and then a fire. The computer terminal was covered in a blanket of black; the monitors slumped, as if they had melted. Shards of papers on the floor, their edges gone, replaced by uneven black borders, also spoke of a fire. Almost to the wall, a large power cable hung from the ceiling; below and surrounding it pooled a blackened stain covering everything from the cable end to the walls, as if it had been severed and poured out oil, coating everything in this part of the lab. He reached down and touched the stain. It had no substance. Then he knew it was soot, from a fire: a flash fire that came from this line, like some sort of lightning bolt, his mind now making sense of the zig-zag patterns that would be more consistent with lightning. Only this lightning had come out of a power cable. *Strange.* Farther up, at the front wall and the far left side of the laboratory, it appeared that the propane tank had exploded. But that fire had remained in that area, from the look of the markings, and was not part of the flash fire that seemed to have blanketed much of the rest of the lab.

At the side office doorway panel, a secret entrance only his wife, Monty, and the builders of his office knew about, he took a deep breath and pushed. It wouldn't give. He pushed harder and it still wouldn't budge. Something must be blocking it on the other side. Then, he noticed them.

Bullet holes? "What the hell?" he bellowed at the obstacle. There were half a dozen bullet holes in the panel he was pushing on, like someone with bad aim had used the wall for target practice. He stepped back and saw that his beloved Keurig—one of his favorite presents from Betsy--had also been the victim of this aggressor's gunfire, a hole in its head. He suspected if he looked he would see the bullet had taken out an empty Donut Shop flavored K-cup, his favorite coffee brand. *Betsy!* His mind returned to the task at hand; he would have to figure out this puzzle later. He bounded up the stairs to the mezzanine walkway and to the double doorway, partially blocked by a desk that had resided farther to the right. More puzzles.

After cleaning and wrapping his wound liberally using the first aid supplies from the supply closet, he grabbed the second set of keys to the truck from the otherwise empty receptionist's desk, and then headed to the side of the building to get the truck and drive to Mendelson's. The first thing he noticed when he left the building was the heat. The sun was high in the sky, indicating it must be noon, but it was as hot a day as he could remember. *It must be the middle of summer.* Turning the corner and expecting to see the white pickup with Stoneridge Research Laboratory painted on its sides, he stopped and stared at an empty space instead.

The truck, like the reception desk, had been intended for staff that he never hired because of his desire to keep his project secret. The truck was to have been driven by a security guard to patrol the fence line and make sure that no one attempted to bother the accelerator tube. But this had turned out to be unneeded as a raised, rounded berm was the only indication of a particle accelerator, protected by an electric fence. And no one seemed too interested in his project aside from his benefactor, a large oil company's investment firm with seemingly endless funds that largely left him alone to develop his clean energy project. No doubt their investment was part of the crazy scheme of earning carbon tax credits for clean-energy investments to counter the global warming tax assessed by the EPA. "Hey, it paid for my project," he would tell Betsy after hearing of a colleague who remarked scornfully that on principle, he would never accept oil money grants.

The missing truck was still curious, as he was the only one who drove it, often using it rather than one of his two personal vehicles. But again, who knew how much time had passed since he had left? *Bicycle*, he thought, remembering that his neighbor along this university warehouse row was an incubator for small businesses and had a garage of bicycles for its enviro-conscious employees. He ducked back into the building and commandeered a few things he thought might be needed, including bolt cutters from the amply outfitted tool and supply closet. Adjusting a new ball cap with SRL embroidered on its front, he trudged the mile or so to go see if he could borrow a bicycle.

Chapter 11
Aug 10 (00:20)

Monty slipped quietly through the back door of his home and then into his office, attempting not to wake his wife. Faraday, their cat, rubbed against his leg and purred loudly, signaling contentment at its master's presence. He plugged in the portable hard drive he had grabbed from Dr. Ron's lab and waited for it to be recognized before he could examine the data. His mind speculated over what had occurred in just the last twenty-four hours, culminating in watching his old friend Dr. Ron travel into time.

"Holy shit!" he whispered loudly. Faraday responded by hopping into his lap, twirling twice and then coming to rest: a little ball of peaceful satisfaction. Monty's fingers tapped away at the keyboard, only stopping every so often to guide his mouse and click here and there. He loaded some of the data into spreadsheets he used for crunching numbers, their formulas calculating and generating answers instantly in their allotted fields. And then he considered the implications.

What had happened was the most incredible thing he had ever witnessed. Dr. Ron actually invented a God-damned time machine and sent himself into the future, and Monty couldn't tell anyone about it. Now the police were after them and somehow, he would have to get back to the lab and send one or two more probes into his future in hopes that Ron would send back data that he received from a medical researcher that Betsy's doctor could use to cure her cancer. *Are we mad?* He scolded himself for having agreed to this. No matter how persuasive Ron's ploys were, it had been Monty's decision to agree to the plan. But everything had been going so fast and his damned friend knew he would be immediately drawn in once he saw the data.

It didn't matter now. He was committed and he had to see this through. He had to find a way back to the lab, get the power turned back on, send in at least one probe and hope that Ron was right.

A movement outside drew his attention away from the computer and out his home-office window. A car pulled up into his driveway and parked beside his Porsche. Monty quickly turned his monitor off, hopeful the driver didn't see him, and watched.

Chapter 12
Aug 10 (00:30)

The man smoothly guided the Escalade, with its headlights off, up onto the drive beside the homeowner's car. The house was completely dark and looked asleep, no doubt just like its occupants. This was going to be one of his easier jobs. He drew a cigarette out of the hard red and silver box, set it between his thin lips, and flicked open the top of his black-lacquered and gold S.T. Dupont lighter. Glimpsing into the pack he saw only two left. He would have to make them last. For now, he would enjoy this one; in the time it would take to smoke it, he'd be able to make sure no one was stirring.

This was his ritual. Just before a kill, he focused on what he knew about his subject, what scenarios might play out, considered even the worst case. Mostly, he relished the moment, enjoying the adrenalin surge that accompanied each kill and knowing that he had power over all things living. It was his one joy in life, and it was something he was good at. This is why he garnered so much for each contract. He had several satisfied clients: the vestiges of the New York mob, although they had mostly dried up; a couple of drug cartels, but he hated working for them; a few politicians, but they were too full of themselves; a few governments, because despite budget cuts, there was always money to take out an enemy; and of course businesses who literally killed their competition. The businesses also paid the best, but they always wanted more than just the kill. They wanted secrets, usually in the form of data his employer desired stolen. This was his specialty, and what made him unique in his field. He took care of the hit and the data collection.

His most recent client had kept him busy with contract after contract, all with tight deadlines, but in return for more and more money. Each time, they never hesitated to pay his price in full to his account in Monaco. It wasn't that he needed the money; he had more than enough saved up for a few lifetimes of blissful retirement at his residence in the south of France, near Cannes. But, what would he do then? Killing people was what he did; it was who he was. If he wasn't doing this, he didn't know what he would do.

It was time. Satisfied he had waited as long as he needed to, and his cigarette almost down to the filter, he flicked it out on the driveway, unconcerned about leaving an evidentiary trail—his DNA would not be found in any database, and rolled up his window.

He stepped out and silently closed the door—the dome light remained off. He had pulled the fuse that controlled the interior lights so that his movement in and out of the vehicle was masked by the darkness. A twist of the suppressor on his FNP-45 Tactical, and he walked to the back of the home.

Chapter 13
Aug 10 (00:40)

Monty opened the door quickly, before the man knocked again, still trying to make sure his wife lay undisturbed—he didn't want her to see what came next. He had watched the man approach the house and although he wasn't sure who he was, he had his suspicions and figured it was time to pay for his part in this mess. The man on the other side thrust something metallic into Monty's face; its shiny surface glistened in the moonlight.

"Detective Johnson with the Dallas Police Department," the voice behind the badge said before he withdrew it. He flipped it back into its case and then continued, "I'm sorry to bother you, sir, at this late hour. Are you Dr. Montgomery Meriweather?"

"Ye-yes, I am," Monty answered. He pulled the door closed behind him so that it would quiet their voices, in case his wife was not awake. His hands were sweaty and unstable. He held onto the door knob for support.

"We are looking for a Dr. Ronald Stoneridge. Have you seen

him?"

"Ah… Not since yesterday. Why, is it his wife?" Monty's voice was abnormally high-pitched, his throat dry. He licked his lips and shuddered slightly.

"You were seen driving away from the"—Johnson pulled out his notepad, found what he was looking for, and continued— "Stoneridge Research Laboratory earlier this evening. Is Dr. Stoneridge with you?"

"You're welcome to come in and look." Monty stepped away from the entrance but kept the door closed, his hand still on the knob, his heart steadying slightly. He might get out of this yet. "I was there this evening. Dr. Ron… I mean, Dr. Stoneridge had called me and asked me to look over his research project at the lab. I was there most of the day with him. I left him there and drove home. I'm just doing some work in my study." He looked at Johnson's eyes and hoped he hid the white lie well enough.

"And what time did you leave Dr. Stoneridge?"

"Ahhh, eight or so. Is he not at his lab? I would imagine he practically lives there."

"He's not there. I'm headed to his home next, but you were on the way."

"That actually makes sense. I'm sure he'll be there, then. His wife Betsy is home sick with the flu or something. I know he wanted to get back home and be with her."

"If he calls you, would you let him know that I have questions for him?"

"I sure will. Have a good evening, detective." After Monty took Johnson's card, he slipped to the other side of the door.

"Good night, Dr. Montgomery," Johnson said, then spun and

walked away to his un-marked car parked in the driveway.

Chapter 14
Aug 10 (00:50)

The man easily unlocked the sliding glass door of Dr. Stoneridge's residence and slid in without making a sound, like a poisonous vapor. He slithered over the tile, the weapon's suppressor leading his search, sweeping back and forth, looking to take any life it could find, like the devil himself collecting his next soul. Although there were none on this first floor.

It appeared to be the standard Western home, with granite counters in the kitchen, which opened up to the dining area and media room with a flat-screen TV; a living room; a separate study; and a guest room. The garage, entered off the kitchen, contained the normal accumulation of junk and one car; the clutter stored beside it confirmed this space wasn't used. With one car in the garage and one parked in the drive, both might be home. A slight smile formed on his spindly lips.

After he cleared the upstairs bedrooms he would return to do a complete search of the computer in the study. If both his target and wife were sleeping, this might turn out to be one of his easiest jobs. He was almost hoping for a little more of a challenge.

He ascended the stairs, careful to step near the wall and railing to avoid the creaking common with most cookie-cutter homes that used nails rather than screws. This one felt a little more solid. Following along the wall past what looked like two guest bedrooms, he stopped before what he assumed to be the master bedroom and listened. An older clock ticked methodically, but he heard no snoring or loud breathing. Either they slept very quietly or they weren't there.

The door creaked slightly as he pushed it open, revealing a king-sized bed containing two hapless shapes. He fired two nearly silent rounds into each form, the spent cartridges landing softly on the carpet. No movement. Sliding past the bed, keeping his eyes on it just in case, he glided over to the master bathroom, its light on and door opened a crack. He listened again, but heard nothing. Nudging this door open more, no creaks this time, he found the bathroom vacant. The bathroom's light splashed upon the bed, revealing it to be empty as well, with a few dead pillows lying under abruptly pulled over covers.

After verifying the other rooms upstairs were empty, the man searched the study. Although nothing on the target's computer looked promising, he made a copy of the computer hard drive on a portable drive he carried with him. The file drawers yielded no further leads. He suspected what he wanted was at his target's laboratory or at his university office. The university would be his next stop.

Twenty-seven minutes after exiting the vehicle he was pulling out of the drive and headed to the campus.

Chapter 15
Aug 10 (01:05)

Peter worried that he had greatly overestimated his sister's longevity to his brother-in-law. When Betsy called in the middle of the night complaining of more chronic pain, he had decided to admit her at Baylor Oncology and order a new series of tests. He suspected they would reveal her condition was worse than he had thought.

And where was Ron? He should be here with her when she needed him most. She kept insisting after he picked her up, "Peter, don't worry about Ron. He's doing what he knows is best for me."

"But where is he?" he asked, trying not to upset her while he drove.

"That's a good question." She paused, holding her head to try and stem the painful drumming. It felt like it might crack open at any moment and she had to hold it together. With the last bit of energy she had left she added, "I can't tell you exactly where or when he is, but I know he's doing what he can for me. Please tell him I love him when you see him." She attempted a feeble smile before passing out, as the shot he'd given her kicked in.

As Pete drove I-75 to Baylor, at a speed faster than he should have, he thought about her words, "I can't tell you exactly where or when he is…" *How odd. Maybe she's already hallucinating.* Now he feared she may only have days rather than months left.

He said a little prayer, even though he wasn't much of a praying man. He asked God for help for his sister: that some answer might be revealed that none of them had yet thought of… For a cure even, no matter how unlikely that might be. His mind then meandered; his thoughts turned to Ron's words, and he wondered what he was planning. He hoped Ron was safe and not breaking the law.

Chapter 16
In The Future

Dr. Ron put the force of his whole body into levering the crowbar wedged between the door frame and the back door, its frame giving, grunting, until *crack*! The door popped open and he sashayed in, no longer concerned about the laws he was breaking or his throbbing hand.

The world he presently occupied was so much worse than the past one, he didn't have the luxury of worrying about antiquated laws like Title 7, Chapter 30 of the Texas Penal Code. Something horrible had happened here and it motivated him to move faster to find Dr. Mendelson, at all costs. What irony that he had used a time machine to get here, but now had this horrible sense of racing against the clock.

When he had left his laboratory yesterday afternoon and traveled the four miles by bicycle, he witnessed a mysterious post-apocalyptic world: none of the cars he pedaled by worked, and all appeared to have been abandoned on the road; all the power seemed to be off, everywhere; and it was much hotter than normal so there were few people wandering around in the midday heat. He had been desperate to find anyone to talk to and discover what the hell had happened and when, still having no idea if he arrived months or years after the moment he stepped through the time slip.

The only person he had spoken to had been darting across his path, barely stopping. When he asked the man what was wrong, the man yelled back, "They're after me" and then promptly jumped off the highway embankment they were both on and disappeared. The second person he ran into literally ran into him. He heard rapid footsteps come from out of nowhere and was pushed from his bicycle. He hit the pavement so hard he passed out watching a big man wearing bib overalls and nothing else pedal away on his bike. More irony, since he had stolen the bike earlier. *Guess it served me right.*

When he came to, the right side of his face felt flushed, probably sunburned. But what shook him to his core were the lights above.

Some years back Betsy and he had been guests on a luxury Alaskan cruise, courtesy of some rich benefactors of his earlier research on gamma ray generation. He had been somewhat reluctant to take the gift, but Betsy had insisted, since they had not had a vacation together in years. One night, outside the Port of Juneau, they watched, mouths agape at the aurora borealis. It was magnificent, and they often talked about what that was like. Now, as he stared straight up at what should have been the dark night sky, what he saw didn't fill him with wonderment. It filled him with dread. The entire sky was carpeted with auroras: red and green undulating currents washing in and out overhead, like some mad psychedelic seascape from Alice in Wonderland. This, of course, was impossible, being this far south of where auroras were ever seen—that is, unless something bad had happened. Then it all fit together: the dead cars, the lack of power, the auroras in the sky, the hotter temperatures. They must have had... rather, were still having a series of calamitous solar storms.

He pushed himself up, wobbling just a little. His mouth was parched and his head pulsed. Something tugged at his shoulder and he was relieved when he saw it was the canvas bag he had been carrying with supplies from his lab, including a bottle of water. He sucked on it like a pacifier, and the plastic crinkled as he pulled out the last drop.

He had guessed he was only a few blocks from Dr. Mendelson's lab, and so he trudged forward on foot, picking up his pace, feeling a little better with each step. He was pushed by a mental tail wind, a need to find this man and with him, his wife's cure.

As if guided by some internal GPS, he reached his destination in a matter of minutes; the bizarre auroras flooded the streets with green-red light, making it easy to see.

Mendelson's lab was in worse shape than his own. In fact, block after block of this area had been consumed by massive fires. More pieces of the puzzle fitted together to provide a more complete picture of what had happened.

After jimmying the door and getting inside, he easily found Mendelson's office, but it was mostly destroyed, and there was nothing salvageable that would lead him to the cure or the man on whom Betsy's life depended. He had one last lead: Mendelson's home. From the mental picture he had of the map, it was about four miles away. He needed to find some more supplies and procure another bicycle, and maybe some sort of weapon.

Stepping outside, he scrutinized the area to get a sense of what was around him to fill his mental shopping list. His head tilted up and once again he was distressed.

Chapter 17
Aug 10 (04:14)

"That was a waste of my time," the man grumbled to himself as he sat back in Dr. Ron's creaky university office chair and considered his next move. The office was meager, filled with a chaotic arrangement of stacked books, typed student reports, and University correspondence. The bookshelves were bursting with volumes about physics, mathematics, quantum mechanics, relativity, thermodynamics, and words the man had never heard of. Randomly poking out from the tangle of books and piles were faculty and science achievement awards, and various knickknacks and trip pictures. Submerged beneath this sea of paper and junk was his target's desk and computer, networked with the university system. None of this yielded anything but a dull headache.

He longed for one of his cigarettes; they helped him think. But he wasn't about to break down and smoke one of his last two just yet, not when it could be a long time before he would be able to find another pack. He hated this piss-ant section of America that didn't sell the things he held so dear, like his Dunhills. Far worse was the ignorance of its people, with their poor taste in clothes and food, their bad accents, and their always wanting to shake his hand. He couldn't stand to touch any of them, even with his gloves on. He tugged on the end of his right Fratelli Orsini, mindful of not stretching the leather too much, and then curled his fists into balls, squeezing tight for a moment, and then exploding his fingers outward as if that could expel the sickness he imagined swarming around his gloved hands.

His phone's buzzing broke his concentration and the silence, agitating him further. The phone's display said the number was "blocked," but there was only one person who would be calling him now.

"Is it done?" His handler's voice was both insistent and whiny.

"No! The package is missing. The police are after him and he is most likely on the run." His words seethed out like the steam from a boiling tea kettle. He should have demanded triple his fee for their putting him through this.

"It is imperative you finish and get the data before the authorities or someone else gets him. We will pay you four times your normal fee, but this must be done by tomorrow at the latest."

"Da," he acknowledged before ending the call and slipping his phone back into his sport coat's inside pocket. He would go back to the doctor's lab and poke around there, police or no police. It was time to push this along. The trail was getting colder.

The man sprang up from his seat and walked to the door. His chair scooted backward across the timeworn linoleum floor, coming to rest against Cindy Spinnaker's body. It was the one day she had come to work early to type up Dr. Ron's notes for his single class, which were to be included in the fall syllabus. Her wide eyes and vacant smile reflected her momentary excitement at thinking her boss had arrived before her--now a frozen flash in time, like a surreal photograph. What looked like a third eye etched into her forehead winked tears of red, which puddled on the floor beneath her.

Chapter 18
Aug 10 (04:15)

Monty inched past building after building, oblivious to their darkness, with the moon providing barely enough light to navigate the frontage road and yet remain unseen. Approaching the lab, he tried to blink back fatigue's clutches on his weary eyes and mind. He replayed today's events and always ended at the same two things that pounded his nerves: Dr. Ron was never coming back, and if he didn't succeed in getting another time slip open, it would have all been for nothing. Fearful of waiting at the house any longer, he figured he would take his chances and hide in the lab, watching for an opportunity to present itself.

The Porsche's tires rolled over the asphalt almost silently as he passed. A beat of hope filled him at seeing only one police car parked out front, yellow police tape pulled across the entrance. No sign of the officer, though, who must have been either inside or patrolling the grounds. Monty couldn't have the officer interrupting him before he could finish—all he needed was fifteen minutes. The building's lighted sign was out and the darkened fence line around back seemed to confirm the complex's power was still off. He had no idea how he would get power back on, assuming as he did that the police or someone from the power company caused this outage by flipping a switch or locking down the meter. If that was all, he just had to figure out where the switch or meter was and then flip it back on. But first, he set up a diversion.

For the second time in less than twenty-four hours, Monty hopped over the fence. He had planned on the electrified barrier being off. What he hadn't planned on was getting stuck on the fence's barbed-wire top. He wasn't paying attention because he was looking past the laboratory complex to other properties and realized that the lights were not on anywhere to the south of the highway for about three blocks. He was noticing this, puzzled and unsure what he would do if he couldn't just flip a switch, when he got stuck. A particularly nasty barb was biting into his arm, drawing a little bead of blood from his forearm. Frozen for a moment, stuck and in plain view of anyone who might look his direction, he decided to try to work his way back to unhook his tangled arm. Then he saw something out of the corner of his eye that terrified him to his core: lights! His head spun around and he watched from his twelve-foot-high perch above the ground in horror as the power was coming on in sections toward him, and very quickly: a square section of lights three blocks away, then two blocks away, then the next block. He panicked and yanked his arm out of the tangled wire, ripping a deep gash between his elbow and wrist. Now free, he turned his shoulders and flexed his knees to jump, when the property's spotlights erupted. Then, like in a slow-motion highlight reel, he was airborne.

~~~

The man pulled the Cadillac off the road at the same place by the billboard and watched. Only one police car sat in front of the lab's entrance, but no one appeared to be in the car. He would only have one, maybe two officers to eliminate and find the data his handlers wanted, and maybe clues to his target's whereabouts. He might even get lucky and have the target show up.

He was about to exit the vehicle, his driver's-side door slightly ajar, when lights started to blink on a few blocks behind the complex and then on and around the complex itself. Pulling the door shut firmly, he watched for movement.

Chapter 19
In The Future

Finding Dr. Mendelson's house was easier than he expected, as he remembered the map's details quite well before his slip through time: all he had written was an address and cross streets to jog his memory; it wasn't like there were public phones with attached phonebooks around anymore to look up addresses. The doctor's unassuming two-story stucco stood in a neighborhood of what looked like two and three-story upper-middle-class homes. It had been a suburban utopia at one time, with manicured lawns and bushy trees, sharp-looking streets crowded with children playing, a paperboy chucking the daily onto driveways, and crossover vehicles racing from garages to get to work, their drivers applying last-minute lipstick or taking sips of their morning coffee. Now it was a scene from a disaster movie or an ongoing nightmare: most of the homes were burned to the ground. The few remaining, like Mendelson's, were looted, with doors open, a scattering of windows broken and various belongings tossed into the yard. It was a soulless place.

Dr. Ron pulled out his hand-scrawled note, inspecting it more closely to make sure he wasn't reading a 1 as a 7 or a 5 as a 6. Betsy always chided him for his poor penmanship, often looking at his handwritten notes and asking, "What does this say?"

"It says 5-1-1-6," he answered, speaking to a black roll-a-board in front of him on the lawn. "This is the place, Bets." And he just stood there, shoulders sagging, heart pumping. He really longed for her and felt regret at leaving her for this lame-brain scheme of his that now looked to have little chance of working. Even when he had told her about his plan, as the words were coming out of his mouth, he had started to question its feasibility: how would he convince this Dr. Mendelson to give him the formula, how would he find him... Endless questions filled his mind. But then his life partner so enthusiastically embraced it, squeezing his hands and telling him, "I trust you, husband, and I know you will be successful." This made the plan real and gave him certainty. A certainty he didn't feel now, looking at this abandoned home.

Perhaps he should have just stayed with her and comforted her in her final hours. At least they would have been together in her last few months... days. Instead, he left her to die alone. That thought stuck at the bottom of his gut; a sour taste of bile tried to work its way up.

His sagging head eyed the doorway, not wanting to go in, afraid that this would be the end of the line, that he wouldn't find this Mendelson. He could see that the man wasn't going to be home, and that most likely there wouldn't be any leads inside. So he just stood there, filled with doubt. This was a rare sensation for him, as doubt never played a part in any of his decisions; he always knew what to do because science guided him. And when he wasn't sure, he retested until he was. Even with matters of the heart and his love for Betsy, it was easy. Their love was something tangible to him, as real as the laws of physics: his love for her guided him in everything related to her.

What would she say right now? A smile built, as the answer came to him. "There's always an answer somewhere. If you haven't found it yet, it's because you weren't looking in the right place. Keep on looking until you find it."

Still straddling the bicycle, he swung one leg over it, letting it drop against the discarded luggage. He repositioned the canvas bag slung around his shoulder, transferring the strap's bit to another part that didn't hurt as badly, and stepped up to the threshold and into the home. If this wasn't it, he'd find another place until he found him.

A boot print dented the faux wood door just above the stylish brass handle, but the frame had received the brunt of the violence and now lay broken and in pieces scattered around the doorway. But then he saw a torn piece of paper taped to the door. The note was meticulously handwritten, its letters prominent and very legible:

June 29 - The day the lights went out

To my daughter Victoria,

I am hopeful that you will see this if I don't find you. I am headed to a place of safety. I left you a note with directions on how to get there. This note allows entry for you and whomever you decide to bring along. It may be the only safe place left on earth. So please put aside your anger at me and go. You'll find the key in its usual place.

I always cared, no matter what you may have believed.

Love,
Dad

"June 29th of what year?" he thought out loud. It had been August 9th when he left his office to travel here. He stepped into the home and first tried to find the note to Victoria.

The kitchen had seen the worst of the looting. Broken dishes, cups, glasses, and various pots and pans were strewn about. There was no note on the counter and he didn't see it on the refrigerator or any sort of bulletin board. But something struck him as odd. It was the usual assortment of things you would expect in a kitchen, but something didn't add up—it just didn't feel right.

He combed the floor in case the note had dropped, but he didn't see anything. Stepping through the detritus, he saw another pile at the back of the kitchen. Boxes and cans of food: broth, tofu, gourmet noodles, pasta shells. "No real food," he said to no one. Perhaps it was no mystery at all. If there was no power, there would be no deliveries to the grocery stores; he had earlier confirmed this thought when he passed a looted grocery store. People would be hungry and would look to other houses for food. Still no note.

Again, that feeling hung on him like a weight. There was something wrong about this place. And then he knew: it was the dust, or rather lack of it. If he was years into the future, the house would be covered in a thick layer of dust, but there was only just a little. He knew by the billboard outside his laboratory, changed methodically every six to twelve months, that the start of this calamity had occurred shortly after he had stepped through the time slip—after that day in what was his past. Now, he knew that this apocalypse hadn't happened years ago, but only weeks or a few months ago. That dread crept up further within him.

He continued his search around the house, head down, searching for the note that would tell him where this "place of safety" was that Mendelson wrote about. Within a minute, he found Mendelson's home office. It was similarly tossed about, with papers and drawers from a desk thrown on the floor. Stepping around the mess, he sat in the man's office chair and pondered where he should look next.

If you haven't found it yet, it's because you weren't looking in the right place. Keep on looking until you find it.

The computer was a dead soldier, as he guessed most computers in the world were now. A thought popped into his mind and he turned his gaze downward, pushing his chair away to see a printer cable running under the semi-transparent chair pad and leading to the credenza behind him, on which sat a small laser printer. There were no pages on top, but part of a page stuck out. The remainder jammed inside the machine. Dr. Ron stood up, opened the back housing, and firmly but carefully pulled out the jammed page. He turned it over and plopped back into the chair, like a deflated balloon.

Although the ink was somewhat smudged, as it hadn't yet been fused to the page, it was a mostly complete satellite picture with a map overlay, like one would find on a typical map program. In the middle was a complex of buildings surrounded by a wall. The marker pointing at the complex was labeled Cicada, and he could see "Boulder" prominently displayed above. On the bottom of the page was a GPS location: 38 32 48.55N 104 52 30.00W.

Chapter 20
Aug 10 (04:35)

Monty woke up stunned and groggy. It may have been seconds or minutes; he wasn't sure how long he had been unconscious, but it couldn't have been too long because he was staring at the same early-morning sky, soon to be pushed aside by the sunrise. The glare from the complex's light-sensitive spotlights was uncomfortable. He must have taken quite a jolt from the fence, but he felt okay otherwise. At least he wouldn't have to figure out how to turn the power back on. He snickered at this thought, lying on his back, staring at the sky, as if he were leisurely stargazing with friends on a warm summer evening.

Worry about being caught and his throbbing arm shook the cobwebs from his head. He leaned up and looked down, chin on chest, and was horrified to see his arm was such a mess. Making quick use of his T-shirt to bandage his bloody arm, he could see it looked worse than it felt.

He made himself small and ran to the back of the complex, aiming for the back door, hoping he hadn't yet been seen. His mind and body, still somewhat wobbly, followed the shadows as they bounced and raced forward and then back each time he crossed the path of the spotlights on either side of the fence. Reaching the rear door to Dr. Ron's office, he was relieved to find it was still unlocked, the way he had left it earlier this morning. It also meant that the police hadn't been back here—another good sign. From a closet Monty grabbed one of Dr. Ron's lab coats and made for the laboratory, his arm now aching. If he could get done what he needed to next, and not get caught, he would have to go get stitches.

Monty looked at his watch, trying to remember when he set up his diversion for the police and wondering when it would go off. *Better get moving.* With some luck, he only had the one police officer to contend with, and that fellow should be occupied by the diversion, assuming he wasn't inside. Monty pulled on the bookcase, just enough to peek into the laboratory. It looked clear. He bounded up the stairs to the double doors and peered through the hardened small windows. No one there, either. After securing the doors, he pushed the nearby desk over, just as Ron and he had done to the outside door yesterday. He ran down the stairs and set up. *Where was the diversion?*

It didn't take long: he only had to slip in the hard drive and prep two drones—he figured he'd be lucky if he had time to open the time slip once: it took just as long to prep two.

Everything was ready. His right forefinger shook in anticipation of his diversion and his aching arm. The diversion… if it ever went off, it was going to be costly to him. He sure hoped it was worth it.

When he heard it, he cringed.

Chapter 21
Aug 10 (04:42)

One moment, a denim blue Porsche 911, Monty's pride and joy, sat quietly near the portion of the fence closest to the frontage road, waiting for its owner to return. In the daylight, it might have been conspicuous, with jumper cables attached to the fence on one end and to a crowbar jammed in the car's fuel port on the other end. But in the darkness of the pre-dawn hours, the soon-to-be-diversion was practically invisible.

The next moment a rolling fireball erupted out of its interior, shooting the German Sonnenland soft-top skyward, a flaming mass that then fell, doing somersaults. The police officer who was now standing post in front of the door of Stoneridge Research Lab nearly fell over, not from the force of the blast, but from being startled. He ran to the blast to offer assistance, afraid someone might have been inside.

~~~

The man bit down hard on his cigarette, his second-to-last one, when the blast erupted almost right in front of him. He realized now that Dr. Stoneridge had set up a diversion and must be in his lab. He tossed out his cigarette, stepped on it, and then stopped as he saw the officer running toward him, the burning car between them.

He calmly strolled toward the running officer, who glared at him, perhaps for not assisting with the burning vehicle. The man lifted his gun hand and squeezed off two silent shots without interrupting his gait. The officer, his mouth and eyes widened with astonishment, bounced backwards, laid out flat on his back. The man slowed only slightly, focusing on the terrified officer's head, and fired the kill shot. Like a gymnast performing a well-practiced routine, he grabbed one of the dead officer's hands and dragged the body off the road, where it wasn't likely to be immediately found.

Then he turned and headed to the laboratory.

Chapter 22
Aug 10 (04:58)

The time slip popped open before him, with its twirling wispy lights and window in the middle. Monty focused, his tongue sticking out slightly as he worked the controller, and guided the drone into it. Flying the damn thing was a bit more difficult than Dr. Ron had made it look and he almost missed the window on his first pass—two seconds.

Immediately, data streamed to the computer, its screen blinking. A small window, its meter application, counted up the total data uploaded in megabytes, its digital counter moving so rapidly it was almost impossible to see any one number. He caught a glimpse of 97.45 rolling by and then focused back on the probe, keeping it steady with the remote controller—four seconds.

He glanced back at the portal and then at the separate window on the screen displaying the live feed on its front and back cameras, looking for anything that would indicate Dr. Ron had left a message—five seconds.

Although the view was not entirely clear, he could easily identify what was on the other side of the portal: it was a lab that could have been a mirror image of this one, only badly damaged and presumably unused for years. That room was brighter now than when Dr. Ron had gone through, and so he could see more. The images from the current video feeds and the previous one showed almost nothing looking back in the direction of the time slip. It was sort of a murky, undulating disruption of light. He fixed his attention on this, but the images were just too blurry, as if the focus on the video camera in that direction needed to be adjusted. This further confirmed their theory that the slip was one-directional, even if it didn't make sense. They had tested this when Dr. Ron had attempted to fly the drone back through the slip unsuccessfully. It was puzzling for sure, as they could send back electronic signals from their video feeds to their sensor data, just not material objects—seven seconds.

He also couldn't let the drone go too far from the window, because he started to lose his controls when he moved it farther than an inch or two from the time aperture—nine seconds.

Just before it closed, Monty saw the corner of the first drone Dr. Ron had sent, before involving him. It looked a little banged up, but otherwise intact. There was definitely no sign of Dr. Ron—ten seconds. The slip closed.

Monty's arms dropped. His uninjured left hand, still clutching the remote, pushed against the computer console for support. He let out a deep sigh and felt his exhaustion take control. If their calculations were correct, the time slip he opened was to a point about three to six months later than when Dr. Ron had jumped forward. He was only sure of one thing at this point: Dr. Ron had not made it back to the lab, and certainly not with any useful data to save his wife. So many questions still unanswered, and perhaps they never would be.

The machine had already powered down completely, part of the program's routine as configured by Dr. Ron. No other sounds, except for the tick-tick-tick of unseen hot metal being cooled by the spray of liquid nitrogen.

He would have to try once more. He put down the remote controller and entered in the new equation to open the next time slip, roughly six more months forward. Thinking once more about the calculation to make sure it was correct, he pressed the Enter key and the machine started up again.

Chapter 23
Aug 10 (05:10)

The man estimated he only had a few minutes to get into the lab and take care of business before the next shift of police would arrive to investigate their missing comrade or reports of the explosion. He could hear a low pulsing noise getting louder and louder, like a giant metronome whose movement was speeding up. He would have preferred a less obvious entrance, but speed was most important here. He fired his silenced weapon once at the u-shaped neck of the Master Lock, hanging from a recently added hasp that secured the doorway. It flopped forward, and then slid off where the shank was broken. Undoing the latch, he pushed open the door, breaking the notice posted over the door and jamb announcing, "This property closed by the order of ERCOT for power violations...." The door swung in only a couple of feet before stopping. The entrance was partially obstructed on the other side. He walked through, his gun leading, combing for any unfortunate person who may have been on the other side.

A loud thrumming noise and flashing lights were coming from behind the double doors in front of him. He stepped quickly to them and peered through one of the two small windows. The laboratory looked vast and deep, multiple stories, with a lower floor below and barely visible. He couldn't see what or who was below the railing in front of him, but there was a strange pulsating light and the top edges of a series of bluish concentric circles, like a large ripple in a blue pond, only this was suspended perpendicular to the ceiling. In front of the door was a desk blocking his entrance.

With a free hand he tried the door. It was locked, so he fired twice at the deadbolt securing the two doors and kicked hard on what appeared to be the more likely of the two to give way. It did.

Chapter 24
Aug 10 (05:12)

"Oh my God!" Monty breathed rapidly, his face locked in a hardened combination of fear and excitement, his eyes burning to make out every word of the message coming to him from the time slip.

A noise above disturbed his concentration. Monty jumped as if shocked and spun his head to the side and up, searching the mezzanine level for the disruption. Another noise, louder this time, although just barely registering above the machine's roar. And there was movement. One of the double doors securing the lab's entrance partially opened, although only the top foot of it was visible.

He returned his focus to the time slip just as it closed. Turning back again, he saw a man standing on top of what must have been the desk he had moved in front of the door to block entry. This man was staring past Monty, probably at the time slip—but now at him. Their eyes locked and Monty knew instantly he was about to become a target. As if confirming that thought, the man raised his hand—gun attached--and aimed at Monty, who dropped below the computer console just as a chunk of the desk whiffed over his head.

Monty waited a second, maybe two, and then carefully craned his head up just past the console desk surface and saw the man running along the mezzanine railing toward the stairwell, which led down to him. Monty sprang up, yanked the portable drive out of the computer and dashed for Dr. Ron's office.

It's amazing, he thought, *how slow you are when you have to run for your life.* It felt like his shoes were made of cement as he pumped his hands and feet toward the panel leading to safety—*if I could just make it.* Another *pffft* and a piece of concrete flooring skidded in front of him. He turned to see his aggressor bounding down the stairs while pointing his gun at him. *Run, Monty, run*, he goaded himself.

The Keurig exploded to his right, its days of delivering cups of flavored coffee ended. Monty pressed his palms forward and hit the panel hard. The door gave way instantly, and he pushed through.

Puff-clink-psssst were the last sounds he heard over his pounding heart before he was pushing on the other side of the bookcase. Based on the sound and from the five-cent tour given earlier by Dr. Ron, he guessed that a propane tank was hit. He had to exit right away, before the whole place exploded.

Just then the lights went out. Monty once again was plunged into darkness inside Dr. Ron's office. Remembering where the desk was, he banged into its side and pushed with all his strength, sliding it alongside the bookcase. He reached into a side drawer of the desk, hopeful the keys were still there where Dr. Ron had tossed them. "Bingo!" Monty now pushed the back end of the desk so that it would be resting lengthwise against the bookcase. Two books erupted out of the shelves, as if to say, "No, that won't be enough." Bits of plywood and plasterboard dust stung his skin. *He's shooting at me from the opposite side!*

More shots popped through, as Monty leapt out of the back door and this time turned right. He ran along the back wall of the building, stopping at the gated exit surrounded by the dead electrical fence. Less than a minute later, Monty was pulling away from the compound when he heard the low boom of the explosion and saw just a small flash of orange light. It was a prelude to the sunrise that would come within an hour.

As he drove away, he knew he was fortunate and wouldn't press his luck again. His wife and he were going to disappear.

Chapter 25
Aug 10 (06:15)

Monty yelled up the stairs for a second time, pleading for his wife to get packed up and ready in less than five minutes. Not stopping, Monty trotted to his office, plugged in the portable drive, opened and froze the video feed of the message, and read in stunned silence. Then he mouthed, "No flipping way!" It was the first time he could really read the words on the message. After a second pass, he knew now what they had to do. Separating the message from the rest of the data, he created two images, printed them, and attached them to an email he sent to Dr. Valdez, Dr. Ron's brother-in-law. He would have to call him on the way as well, sure that just an email wouldn't be enough to convince him to do what the message said. He could hardly believe it himself.

After thinking for a moment, Monty burned a copy of all of the data and images onto a spare flash drive. This he sealed it in a bubble mailer, slapped on it a pre-paid label generated from a stamp program, and readied it to be sent in the mail to a colleague at MIT.

Perhaps it was insurance, or maybe he just didn't want this accomplishment to be lost.

His next action he had thought out when he had raced home. Although not sure it would work, it was the best he could do in the time he had remaining. So after shutting down his computer, he opened the side and pulled out the hard drive. He looked around and smiled, finding what he needed next: it was an award he received from the National Academy of Sciences, displayed proudly on a prominent table. Brandishing it like a sledge hammer, he bashed in the side of the drive, pulled out the disc, and ran out of the office. While he was en route to the kitchen, his wife announced, "I'm ready."

The microwave was set on ten minutes, the disc resting inside on the microwave cover, when he pressed the button.

"I'm right behind you."

~~~

The black Escalade didn't hesitate or seek obscurity in the shadows. It pulled up the drive resolutely and stopped behind a white pickup truck--its driver-side door left open by its hurried driver.

The flash of his blue-flamed torch, designed for inflicting pain on cigars, was applied to his last cigarette. Instead of savoring its burn, he took one violent puff and stepped out of the vehicle. His face, red from burns, scowled at his target's house. A deep gash on the right side of his face was held together with a piece of duct tape. Two small rivulets of crimson seeped from its binding and skipped over the stubble of his normally clean face; it would be the closest he would come to shedding tears for this next victim.

But then, beyond the truck, the garage door was left open, empty of all vehicles, telling him they had left already.

He stepped through, just as the owner would after a day at work. After entering the house, he withdrew his weapon, no longer bothering with the silencer. A sound alerted him to the kitchen. It was the microwave, cooking something that was sparking inside, the display telling him there were only five minutes twelve seconds until its contents were ready. He punched the door button with his forefinger knuckle and the door squeaked open to reveal the disc of a hard drive on top of a plastic microwave dish. It was warm, but otherwise salvageable. His handlers might not be entirely upset with his work after all.

~~~

"Where are we going?" his wife asked, as Monty tossed the bubble mailer into the mail drop.

"To our cabin in Arizona."

"Right now?"

"Yes, and you can't tell anyone that we're there."

"Fine. How long will we be there?"

Monty looked at his phone's calendar, did the math and said, "Ten months, sixteen days."

She shifted the cat-carrier from her lap to the back seat. Faraday was already asleep, as if he knew it would be a long drive. "Then what?"

"We're driving with Dr. Ron's wife Betsy and his brother-in-law Peter to a place in Colorado called Cicada."

Chapter 26
In The Future

The sun stood over him like a big bully in a schoolyard, having its way with him and those who were foolish enough to venture outside. Even though fall was supposedly just around the corner, there appeared to be no end to this sweltering heat.

Dr. Ron tied a bandana around his head to protect it against the sun's punishing rays, secured his satchel of supplies around his shoulder and peddled back to his own laboratory. His peddling was methodical but unenthusiastic. He knew where Dr. Mendelson was now—at least where he was headed—but Colorado was a long way away on a bicycle. Even if he could make it in this harsh environment, how would he find this man, get the cure and get back in time for the one or two probes Monty might be able to send? No, his mission was a failure. He would at least tell his friend what he could expect in the present-day world, coming for them in less than a year. He would ask him to try and send another probe or two, but suspected he would be prevented by others from doing so: Monty would be lucky to stay out of jail after getting just one probe back through the time slip right after him.

He kept thinking about his decision to come here and leave Betsy.

The heat sucked up his energy and made his mind wander back to the same memory. Maybe it was the heat, or maybe it was something else...

It was their 20th anniversary dinner, at Betsy's favorite restaurant, The Saltgrass Steak House. They were sipping their glasses of Cabernet when he told her his concerns about their current work.

"I've come to a decision," he said tentatively, as he watched her delight in the taste of her wine.

"What's that, Doctor?" She always referred to Ron this way when he made a serious proclamation.

He grinned at her playfulness and relished how she looked at him, with joyful love and seriousness all at once. "I'm afraid of where we've gone with our research. We know that we can generate an almost unlimited amount of gamma radiation with minimal power usage. But what we hadn't considered are the implications. If this technology were to get into the wrong hands, imagine what could happen." He paused to take a sip of his own wine.

"Someone could create a big green Hulk that would smash everyone in sight, right?" She beamed at him.

He had told her his concerns about the release of too much gamma radiation—the output of the technology they had created-- and what it might do to the earth's magnetic fields. He had reminded her about his ideas to generate clean power using the same technology, and he had already received an agreement from their backers. She had agreed and they toasted some more.

That night, they had talked about his plans to create the same collider that sent him through time. If she hadn't supported it, he wouldn't have traveled through time to save her, and failed. It was her agreement, and the fact that his old lab had been burgled and vandalized that same evening: all his computer equipment and all his research notes were stolen…

Ron almost drove past his building, his mind hanging onto something that escaped him.

He pulled up to the lab and rested his bike on the ground before going in. Once inside, he stopped at the railing and looked out over the giant laboratory, wrecked from an explosion and scarred by fire. He wondered if a time slip would ever be created again in his lifetime, or the next.

Then he noticed it, right past the middle of the two accelerator tubes. It looked like a propped up white board, with writing on it.

He trotted down the stairs and then to the back of the lab, coming to a stop in front of the white board. He had planned on using it to write his own message. And yet there it was, a message already written on it. The first words stunned him. He fell to his knees, as if his legs could no longer bear his weight. His face quivered, his eyes filled with tears and he gulped a breath of air and held it. Finally, he finished reading the words and cried tears of joy. He wiped his eyes with his sleeves and reread the message once more, to make sure he hadn't missed anything. It was definite.

He looked upward, closed his eyes and mouthed the words, "Thank you." He hopped up, as nimble as a sixteen-year-old, and his mind turned over what items would go on his next shopping list. He was about to bike hundreds of miles, to someplace in Colorado. And although he would be tired, he would find the energy. He was going to go see his wife again.

Chapter 27
June 27th

After ten months and seventeen days of hiding, their wait was at an end.

Monty drove past the sign in the middle of the road announcing, "Welcome to Cicada" and pulled up to the large gate. Sounds of their anxiety filled the cab of Monty's Explorer.

Until today, they had spent untold hours discussing their plans after getting the message from the future. "What do you do with this foreknowledge?" was their greatest debate. "How do you sit on something that may save millions, but might cause harm to those who delivered the message to them?" was another biggie. In the end, Monty was the most persuasive and they agreed on the plan, to wait until this day and then drive here.

The waiting was the hardest, the long days spent in solitude in the Arizona White Mountains, while the world went about their daily activities. It allowed their minds to harbor doubt, and that laid waste to their surety of purpose. By the time this day rolled around, they all questioned the reality of the message, in spite of all they witnessed: the retelling and presentation of the data Monty saved was convincing, but above all, it was Betsy's miraculous turnaround. And yet, the waiting ate at their resolve and all wondered, *Would the Event really come on June 28th?* But yesterday evening's very abnormal auroral light show seemed to confirm its probability. *Would this place they were going to go to even exist?* And yet, here they were, parked in front of Cicada.

The gates creaked open and the vehicle's occupants watched in anticipation of what would come next.

~~~

They were all seated around a giant cherry conference table, in sumptuous leather chairs on rollers, more like being in the board room of some giant Fortune 500 company than the conference room of a remote research facility.

"So, Dr. Montgomery, why don't you start from the beginning and tell me why you are here," asked Preston with a tone that was more command than query. He was the head of the facility and the man they had been told to seek out.

"Please call me Monty. May I call you Preston?"

"Yes, fine."

"Tomorrow, the world will experience the worst solar storm in recorded history. The Event, as it will be known, will not only turn out the lights, but kill much of the world's population." Monty watched for Preston's reaction: his face remained stoic, the statement eliciting none of the shock, or at least disbelief, Monty expected. "You don't seem surprised." The words were merely a verbalization of his suspicion that Preston somehow knew what was coming.

"You haven't answered how you found out about Cicada and what you are doing here." Preston's tone now confirmed Monty's suspicion. He knew already.

Monty opened his satchel and withdrew two stapled pages he had printed, each containing the imbedded screen-shots of the meticulous handwriting on a whiteboard: the message that sent them here. The first page said,

> My name is Dr. Greg Mendelson. I am writing this for two reasons: first to warn you of an impending apocalypse that will hit you on June 28th and second to give you the cure to Betsy Stoneridge's cancer. You will find the formula for an experimental drug we have found to be 100% effective in all of our early tests against most forms of cancer.

> I am not prone to flights of fancy, yet here I am, after being told that I would write this at this point in the future, to warn others in the past. Paradoxical improbabilities aside, I knew this to be real when I was told "Luxembourg1989"--my computer password--as the place and date I met my wife, now deceased from cancer.

> A giant solar storm will cause mass deaths and collapse the world's economies. After this, one of the few places of hope left will be Cicada, a place from which I received much of my grant funding for my pandemic research that led accidentally to my cancer research.

> To all who read this:

> Get the formula below to Dr. Valdez immediately, but have him bring his patient to a safe place where he can still produce this and administer it. Results will occur almost immediately, and a complete recovery can be expected within days, assuming there was not too much cellular damage to her other organs.

Preston flipped the page abruptly, his mouth slightly ajar. This, he didn't expect.

You are to tell no one about this, even though you will be tempted to do so. You risk changing what has already occurred. And although it may mean you will save a few people temporarily, they will ultimately die anyway because there is no escaping what is to come. BEWARE! There are also enemies about, who would kill you to get this info. So protect yourselves and stay in hiding and on June 27th, the day before the Event, present yourselves to Preston at Cicada (38 32 48.55N & 104 52 30.00W). Tell him "Stephanie has blue eyes" and he will let you in.

Preston looked up from the page with a *what-the-hell?* gaze that burnt holes into Monty, before returning to reading.

Then show him this message. Tell him your qualifications and he should let you stay. Finally, when I arrive at Cicada, with my invitation, seven days later, show me this message so that I'll be convinced to write it.

To Dr. Valdez, here is the formula:
One part: $C_{27}H_{29}NO_{11}$ to 4 parts: $C_{17}H_{26}O_4$
administered in doses of 500 milligrams once per day for two weeks.

Preston flipped back to the first page and read the whole message again. He thought for a moment before looking up at Monty. "How did you come by this information?"

"This is the part that will be hard to believe."

Preston snorted. "That's probably an understatement. Go ahead."

"Well, my friend invented a machine that creates a controlled time slip, allowing him to monitor and get data from the future, and"—Monty hesitated, then continued—"and allowing travel forward to that future point, through the time slip."

"So where is this Dr. Ron?" Preston asked and then answered his own question, in a snarky tone. "No, let me guess, he's jumped back into the future in his trusty Delorean?"

Monty chuckled too, picturing Dr. Ron dressed like Michael J. Fox in the 1980s hit. "I know this is hard to believe. If I hadn't witnessed it myself, I wouldn't have believed it." He pulled out the portable hard drive. "However, I have all of the research and test data here. Let me show you and any of your scientists the proof."

~~~

July 1st

"Dr. Gregory Mendelson," he said, extending his hand. "Preston says you know me and wanted to see me." He glanced over at Betsy and Dr. Vasquez and pumped Monty's hand.

"No, we've never met but I have a story to tell you that affects you—well, all of us. I believe you'll want to sit down before I share it." Monty motioned Mendelson to the same conference table where they had shown Preston the same message not long before. Monty slipped the pages across the table.

Mendelson took the news in stride, and after seeing his unique handwriting and speaking with Betsy and Dr. Vasquez, he knew the story to be real. He told them about the miracle cure that never made it to trials, as they were interrupted by the Event. He told him he was one of the scientists chosen for Cicada because he had suspicions that the world's end would come as a result of genetic manipulations to fast-growing cancer cells. It was for this that he received funding from Cicada.

Next, they had to convince Mendelson to go, but he was the one that posed the question back to them. "The bigger question is what would happen if I didn't go? This would cause an enormous paradox, because if I don't go, how could I have written that message to begin with? And if I didn't write that message, Betsy wouldn't be alive and you wouldn't be here."

Mendelson agreed and then excused himself. His daughter Victoria had made it two days earlier, with her family, and he wanted to spend a little time with them before leaving the next morning. Betsy stopped him before he left and said, "May I ask you a big favor?" Her eyes begged him.

"For you, of course." He smiled a genuine smile that reached clear up to his eyes.

"Would you leave this note for my husband below your message?" She thrust a piece of paper that was folded in quarters and stapled. On the front she had written in cursive, "To my Dearest Husband Ron."

"I would be honored." He took the note and kissed her hand. Then he looked up at her and said, "You know I'm going because of you? Your being alive is the culmination of my life's work. I told my wife long ago, before she died, that if I could save just one person with my work, it would be worth it. Besides, I'm hopeful that your husband will find my message and now your message and will make it to Cicada and you. Maybe you both will get the second chance I never did with my wife."

Chapter 28
Sometime Later

He pedaled at breakneck speed, almost losing his balance twice on the loose gravel, fueled by excitement and adrenaline. In spite of his muscles screaming in pain, he wasn't about to relent now. It had taken him almost a month, although it felt longer, to bike the eight hundred miles. He was aware that his body showed the effects of all of those miles, not the least of which was that for the first time in his life, he was skinny--probably too skinny. But after a long journey and not eating at all some days because he couldn't find food, that was to be expected. None of that mattered today as he steadied himself once more, almost going down again. He had somehow made it this far, and soon, maybe in a few minutes, he would see his wife.

His mind repeated the words from her note, left for him below the white board, with Greg Mendelson's Sharpie attached to it--he almost didn't see it with all the other debris, "I will watch and wait for you, that day you come back to me. That day will be the happiest day of my life."

He hit the brakes, slid to a stop, and looked up at the massive gate. He wasn't sure what to do next, so he yelled out, "Hello?"

After waiting a little longer, he yelled out again, "Hello, is anyone there? This is Doctor Ronald Stoneridge. I have traveled eight hundred miles to see my wife Betsy. Is she there? Hello?"

After a moment, the gates opened. They swung in and stopped, leaving just enough room for a single person. And then he saw her standing there, her arms outstretched toward him. It would be his happiest day as well.

Epilogue

Rodney Deerwester turned the bubble mailer around in his hands, inspecting it with the greatest curiosity. He stared at his name and address printed from some stamp program. There was no name on the return, only an address in Dallas, Texas. He only knew one person from Dallas, and that was his old friend Monty, who was horrible at keeping touch and whom he hadn't corresponded with in years.

"Sign here," demanded "Mr. Smiley," the name the kids called him because he never smiled.

Rodney scrawled his name on the electronic pad, his writing almost unintelligible. "Thanks, Bob," he said to the mopey postal worker and left, already zipping open the top of the mailer. Rodney stopped at the garbage by the exit, discarding the stringy piece and intending to dump the envelope too. He turned it over and gave it a flick to dislodge its contents. A stainless steel stick skidded out into his awaiting palm, but nothing else. He looked inside, thinking a note should be there, but there was nothing. Tossing the envelope in the trash, he pushed the flash-drive around his palm, as if he expected it to come alive and tell him its purpose. The mystery would have to wait. He had to get to the Y, then he had to give his class, and then maybe he could load the contents into his computer and find out the answer to this mystery.

He shoved the stick into the pocket of his warmups and walked down Massachusetts Avenue to the YMCA.

~~~

The man blew out a long cloud of smoke, dropped the cigarette on the ground, and drove his heel into it, extinguishing it completely. A woman walking toward him looked up, her face dark with scorn, her lips preparing to launch a tirade of words about his littering and smoking in public. Then she saw his face, and her scorn transformed into surprise and then terror. She wanted to look away, sure she was seeing evil in person, but her gaze was stuck on the man's features: the long vertical scar on his cheek, the scabbed-over areas of his head, the hair mostly absent on one side, the thin lips that curled into a smile and those eyes, dark as a nightmare.

The man glanced past her, ignoring her altogether, as his gaze followed his target; he was headed to the Y to do his workout. Finally, he had gone to his box and picked up the package. The man had watched his target dump a stick drive in his palm and discard the envelope, before shoving the drive into his pants pocket. It was the stick he was after… Simple. Then that would be the end of this whole Stoneridge-Merriweather affair.

Read what happens next in *The Stick* (Coming in the future).

Did you like *Time Slip*?

Please leave a Review

stoneageseries.com/short2

Reviews are vital to indie authors. If you liked this book, I would really appreciate your review

Thank you!

Want to join in discussions about *Time Slip*?

Positive or negative comments, it doesn't matter. Join the discussion here: stoneageseries.com/about/time-slip/

FREE EBOOK

Max's Epoch
- A Stone Age Short

Get the exclusive novella about *Stone Age's* #1 character, Max Thompson

Sign up for *ML Banner's Apocalyptic Updates* (Readers list) and get a free copy of the exclusive novella (not available on Amazon or any other book sales channel), *Max's Epoch – A Stone Age Short.* Just who is Maxwell "Max" Thompson? You know him as a prepper and close friend of the Kings, but why? What happened in Iraq? Who's bugging his phones? Who's after him? These questions and more are answered in the new exclusive *Stone Age Short.*

Get your copy here:
MLBanner.com/free

Where is the Stone Age World?

Time Slip take place in the world described in the *Stone Age Series* and launched in April 2014 with the #1 Amazon apocalyptic-thriller,
STONE AGE.

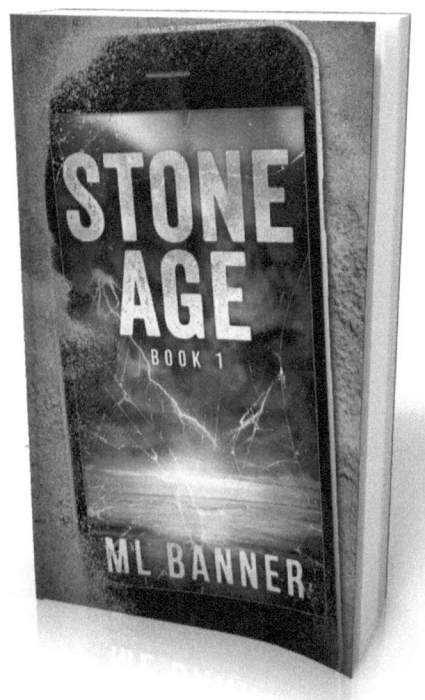

The greatest solar storm in recorded history is coming again, and when it does it will send the earth back to a technological new Stone Age.

A family on a Mexican vacation gets separated.
A self-proclaimed prophet's fame grows.
A scientist sends out a final ignored warning.
An astronaut is stranded on the International Space Station.

Lives are lost, survivors persevere, and new heroes are born. All
will question if the Event signals the end,
or the beginning of something much worse.

Pick up the story that has been read by over 50,000 people.

READ *STONE AGE* TODAY
(Available on Amazon)

Who is ML Banner?

Michael "ML" Banner is an award winning, international best-selling author of apocalyptic thrillers.

Three of his six published books were #1 Amazon best-sellers in one or more genres. Highway won the 2016 Readers Favorite Gold Medal in Thrillers and 2016 Finalist for Kindle Book Review's Best Sci-Fi Novel. His work is traditionally published and self-published.

A serial entrepreneur, having formed multiple of businesses over the years. He founded and still dabbles in SmallBiZ.com which helps small businesses form and maintain entities, forming almost 100,000 entities over its 17 years of existence.

When not running a business or writing his next book, you might find Michael hunting, traveling abroad, or reading a Kindle with his toes in the water (name of his publishing company) in the Sea of Cortez (Mexico). That's because he and his wife split time between their homes in Tucson and on a beach in Mexico.

Want more from M.L. Banner?

MLBanner.com

Receive FREE books &

Apocalyptic Updates - A monthly publication highlighting discounted books, cool science/discoveries, new releases, reviews, and more

Keep in Contact – *I would love to hear from you!*

Email: michael@mlbanner.com
Google+: google.com/plus/+mlbanner
Facebook: facebook.com/authormlbanner
Twitter: @ml_banner

www.ingramcontent.com/pod-product-compliance
Lightning Source LLC
Chambersburg PA
CBHW052014170626
46808CB00007B/2921